THE PEOPLE
WHO
HUGGED
THE TREES

AN ENVIRONMENTAL FOLK TALE

adapted by Deborah Lee Rose
from a story of Rajasthan, India
with pictures by Birgitta Säflund

HBJ Harcourt Brace Jovanovich, Inc.
Orlando Austin San Diego Chicago Dallas New York

As a part of HBJ TREASURY OF
LITERATURE, 1993 Edition, this edition is
published by special arrangement with
Roberts Rinehart Publishers.
Grateful acknowledgment is made to
Roberts Rinehart, Inc. Publishers, P. O. Box
666, Niwot, CO 80544 for permission to
reprint *The People Who Hugged the Trees*
by Deborah Lee Rose, illustrated by
Birgitta Säflund. Text copyright © 1990 by
Deborah Lee Rose; illustrations copyright
© 1990 by Birgitta Säflund.
Printed in the United States of America
ISBN 0-15-304601-5
2 3 4 5 6 7 8 9 10   059   96   95   94   93

FOR MIRANDA
who loves the trees
DLR

FOR JOAKIM & PAOLA
BS

Special thanks to David Magier, PhD,
South and Southeast Asia Bibliographer, Columbia
University

In long-ago India, when warrior princes ruled the land, there lived a girl who loved the trees. Her name was Amrita.

Amrita lived in a poor village of mud houses, on the edge of the great desert. Just outside the village grew a forest.

Every day Amrita ran to the forest, her long braid
dancing behind her. When she found her favourite tree,
she threw her arms around it. "Tree," she cried, "you
are so tall and your leaves are so green! How could we live
without you?" For Amrita knew that the trees shaded her from
the hot desert sun. The trees guarded her from the howling desert
sandstorms. And where the trees grew, there was precious water to
drink. Before she left the forest, Amrita kissed her special tree.
Then she whispered, "Tree, if *you* are ever in trouble,
I will protect you."
The tree whispered back
with a rustle of its leaves.

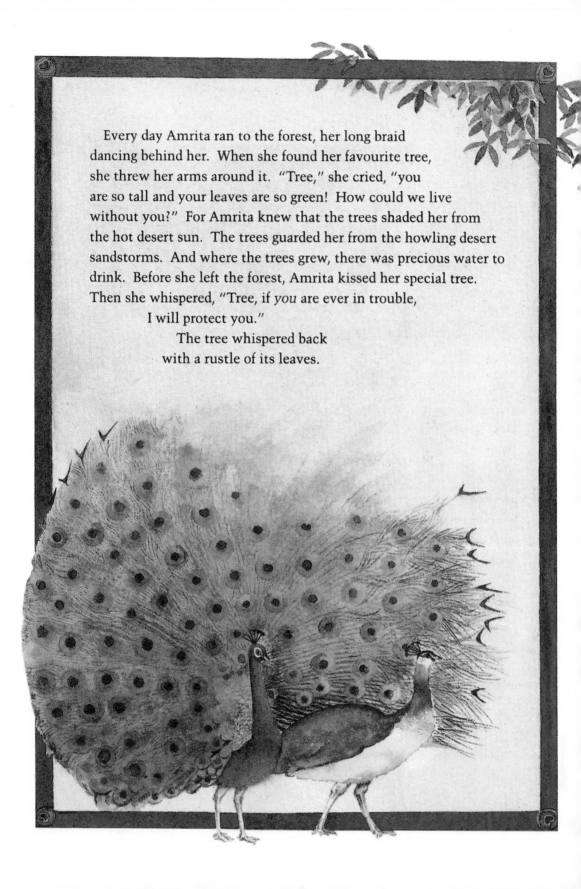

One day just before the monsoon rains, a giant sandstorm
whirled in from the desert. In minutes the sky turned dark as
night. Lightning cracked the sky and wind whipped the trees as
Amrita dashed for her house. From inside, she could hear the
sand battering against the shutters. After the storm ended, there
was sand everywhere—in Amrita's clothes, in her hair and even
in her food.

But she was safe and so was her village, because the trees had
stood guard against the worst of the storm.

As Amrita grew, so did her love for the trees. Soon she had her own children, and she took them to the forest with her.

"These are your brothers and sisters," she told them. "They shade us from the hot desert sun. They guard us from the terrible desert sandstorms. They show us where to find water to drink," she explained. Then Amrita taught her children to hug the trees as she did.

Each day when she left the forest, Amrita fetched water from the village well. She carried the water in a large clay pot, balanced on top of her head.

One morning
by the well, Amrita
spotted a troop of men armed with
heavy axes. They were headed toward
the forest. "Cut down every tree you can find," she
heard the chief axeman say. "The Maharajah needs
plenty of wood to build his new fortress."

The Maharajah was a powerful prince who ruled over
many villages. His word was law. Amrita was afraid.
"The tree-cutters will destroy our forest," she thought.
"Then we will have no shade from the sun or protection
from the sandstorms. We will have no way to find
water in the desert!" Amrita ran to the forest and hid.
From her hiding place, she could hear the *whack* of the
axes cutting into her beloved trees.

Suddenly Amrita saw the chief axeman swing his
blade toward her special tree.

"Do not cut down these trees!" she cried and jumped in front of her tree. "Stand back!" thundered the axeman. "Please, leave my tree," Amrita begged. "Chop me instead." She hugged the tree with all her strength. The axeman shoved her away and swung his blade.

He could see only the tree he had been ordered to cut. Again and
again the axeman chopped until Amrita's tree crashed to the ground.
Amrita knelt down, her eyes filled with tears. Her arms tenderly
grasped the tree's dying branches.

When news of Amrita's tree reached the village, men, women and children came running to the forest. One after another they jumped in front of the trees and hugged them. Wherever the tree-cutters tried to chop, the villagers stood in their way.

"The Maharajah will hear of this!" threatened the chief axeman.

But the people would not give in.

The Maharajah was furious when the axemen returned emptyhanded. "Where is the wood I sent you to chop?" he stormed. "Your Highness, we tried to cut down the trees for your fortress," answered the chief axeman. "But wherever we went, the villagers hugged the trees to stop us."

The Maharajah sliced the air with his battle sword. "These tree-huggers will pay for disobeying me!" He mounted his fastest horse and rode out for the forest. Behind him came many soldiers, riding long-legged camels and elephants with jeweled tusks.

The Maharajah found the people gathered by the village well.

"Who has dared to defy my order?" he demanded. Amrita hesitated a moment, then she stepped forward.

"Oh Great Prince, we could not let the axemen destroy our forest," she said. "These trees shade us from the baking desert sun. They protect us from the sandstorms that would kill our crops and bury our village. They show us where to find precious water to drink."

"Without these trees I cannot build a strong fortress!" the Maharajah insisted.

"Without these trees we cannot survive," Amrita replied.

The Maharajah glared at her.

"Cut them down!" he shouted.

The villagers raced to the forest as the soldiers flashed their swords. Step by step the soldiers drew closer, as the sand swirled around their feet and the leaves shivered on the trees. Just when the soldiers reached the trees the wind roared in from the desert, driving the sand so hard they could barely see.

The soldiers ran from the storm, shielding themselves behind the trees. Amrita clutched her special tree and the villagers hid their faces as thunder shook the forest. The storm was worse than any the people had ever known. Finally, when the wind was silent, they came slowly out of the forest.

Amrita brushed the sand from her clothes and looked around. Broken tree limbs were scattered everywhere. Grain from the crops in the field littered the ground.

Around the village well drifts of sand were piled high, and Amrita saw that only the trees had stopped the desert from destroying the well and the rest of the village.

Just beyond the well the Maharajah stood and stared at the forest. He thought for a long time, then he spoke to the villagers.

"You have shown great courage and wisdom to protect your trees. From this day on your trees will not be cut," the Maharajah declared.

"Your forest will always remain a green place in the desert."

The people rejoiced when they heard the Maharajah's words. They sang and danced long into the night and lit up the sky with fireworks.

In the forest, the children strung flowers and bright colored paper through the branches of the trees. And where Amrita's tree had fallen, they marked a special place so they would never forget the tree's great sacrifice.

Many years have passed since that day, but some people say Amrita still comes to the forest to hug the trees.

"Trees," she whispers, "you are so tall and your leaves are so green! How could we live without you?"

For Amrita knows that the trees shade the people from the hot desert sun.

The trees guard the people from the howling desert sandstorms.

And where the trees grow there is water, and it is a good place for the people to live.

In the original legend, Amrita Devi and several hundred villagers gave up their lives while protecting their forest, nearly three centuries ago. The Indian government has commemorated their sacrifice by naming the Rajasthani village of Khejare as India's first National Environment Memorial.

Today, the people of India still struggle to protect their environment. One of the most dedicated groups is the Chipko ("Hug the Tree") Movement, whose members support nonviolent resistance to the cutting of trees.

In 1987, the Chipko Movement received the distinguished Right Livelihood Award (the "alternative Nobel"), for "dedication to the conservation, restoration, and ecologically responsible use of India's natural resources."